D0257437

For my brother Tian,
who endured many an itchy jumper
from our own knitting Nana x

First published in Great Britain in 2017 by Fourth Wall Publishing

ISBN: 978-1-910851-45-6

www.fourthwallpublishing.com
2 Riverview Business Park, Shore Wood Road, Bromborough, Wirral, Merseyside CH62 3RQ
A catalogue record for this book is available from the British Library.
Printed in China.

My
INCREDIBLE
Knitting
NANA
by Rowena Blyth

My Nana **loves** to knit.
She just can't help herself.

She knits me
warm woolly jumpers...

hats and gloves...

and scarves that cover
my head!

She knits me teddies
and toys...

coats for the cat...

and even a
toilet roll doll!

Slip, knit, pass and pearl is all I hear at Nana's house.

So one very cold winter, as we watched a programme
about the blizzards in Antarctica, it came as no surprise when Nana said,

"Look at those poor little penguins, all huddled together in the cold.
I must knit them some jumpers right away – Molly, grab my wool – **let's go!**"

Without a second thought, we were boarding a plane
to the penguins' home on the ice.

When we arrived in Antarctica,
we all stood in shock,
we couldn't **believe** what we saw!

Not a small group of penguins, but **two hundred** or more,
all shivering and shaking and cold.

Nana got knitting right away!

**Slip, knit, pass and pearl,
slip, knit, pass and pearl...**

...until they all had
warm woolly jumpers.

But then...

...A whale on his travels
popped his head up to say,
"I see you've been busy.
I don't suppose you'd
knit me a hat?"

Before Nana knew it, word had spread and a **long queue** started to form.

Poor Nana was **frazzled!** But she kept on knitting,
until the whole of Antarctica was warm.

"Onwards we go!" said Nana.
"There's still **so much** left to do."
Thank you!

And with that, Nana **knitted** and **stitched**,
looped and **clicked** her way all around the world.

From London... to Paris... to New York... and Rome.

She barely dropped a stitch.

On to Russia...

and China...

Greenland...

and Japan.

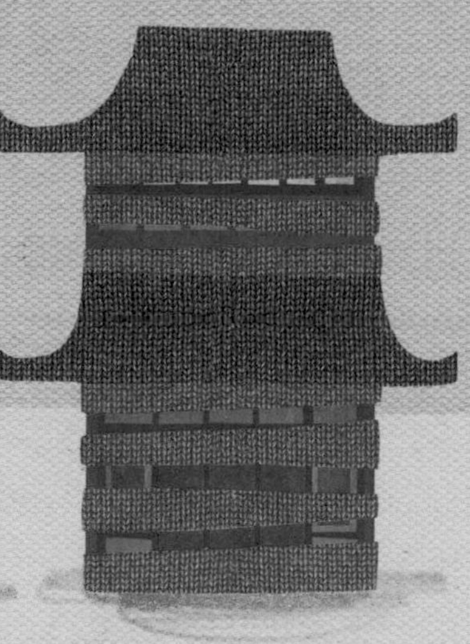

Nana's mission was gathering pace.

Soon, things got
a little out of hand...

HumpbackWhaleOrcaWhale
KingPenguinBlueWhale
KelpGullEmperorPenguin
LeopardSealAntarcticFur
SealCrabeaterSealHusky
WanderingAlbatrossBigBen
EiffelTowerStatueOfLiberty

ColosseumAmphitheatre
St.Basil'sCathedralGreatWall
OfChinaIglooSensō-jiTemple
StonehengeLeaningTowerof
PisaMountFujiTajMahal
EgyptianPyramidsSydney
OperaHouseChichénItzá
GoldenGateBridge

Slip, knit, pass and pearl
could be heard for miles around.

Before long, the **whole world** could be seen from outer space as a **gigantic** ball of wool!

Then one warm day,
it started to rain...
and rain...
and rain...

and rain.

...the whale was **winding**...
...the huskies
were **hauling**...

Everyone came to help,
and the great unravelling began.

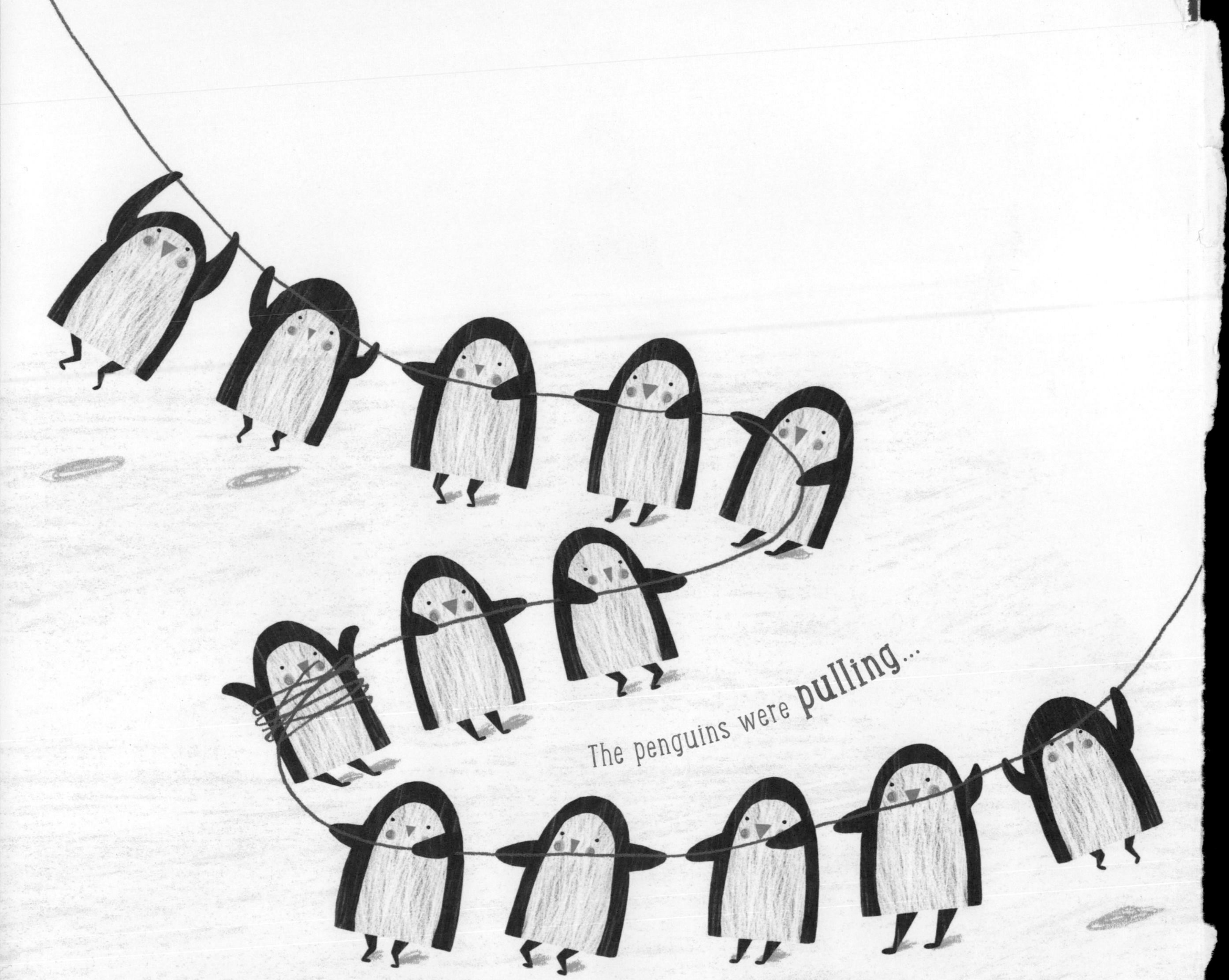

The penguins were **pulling**...

Until one by one, **everything** Nana had knitted began to...

shrink...

and squeeze...

and squeak!

"Oh no!" cried Nana.
"We must act fast,
before the whole world
starts to shrink!"

"Don't worry," I said,
"I have a plan. We just need
to call some old friends."

...until Nana's bag was **full!**

...the birds
were **bundling**...
...the seals were **sorting**...

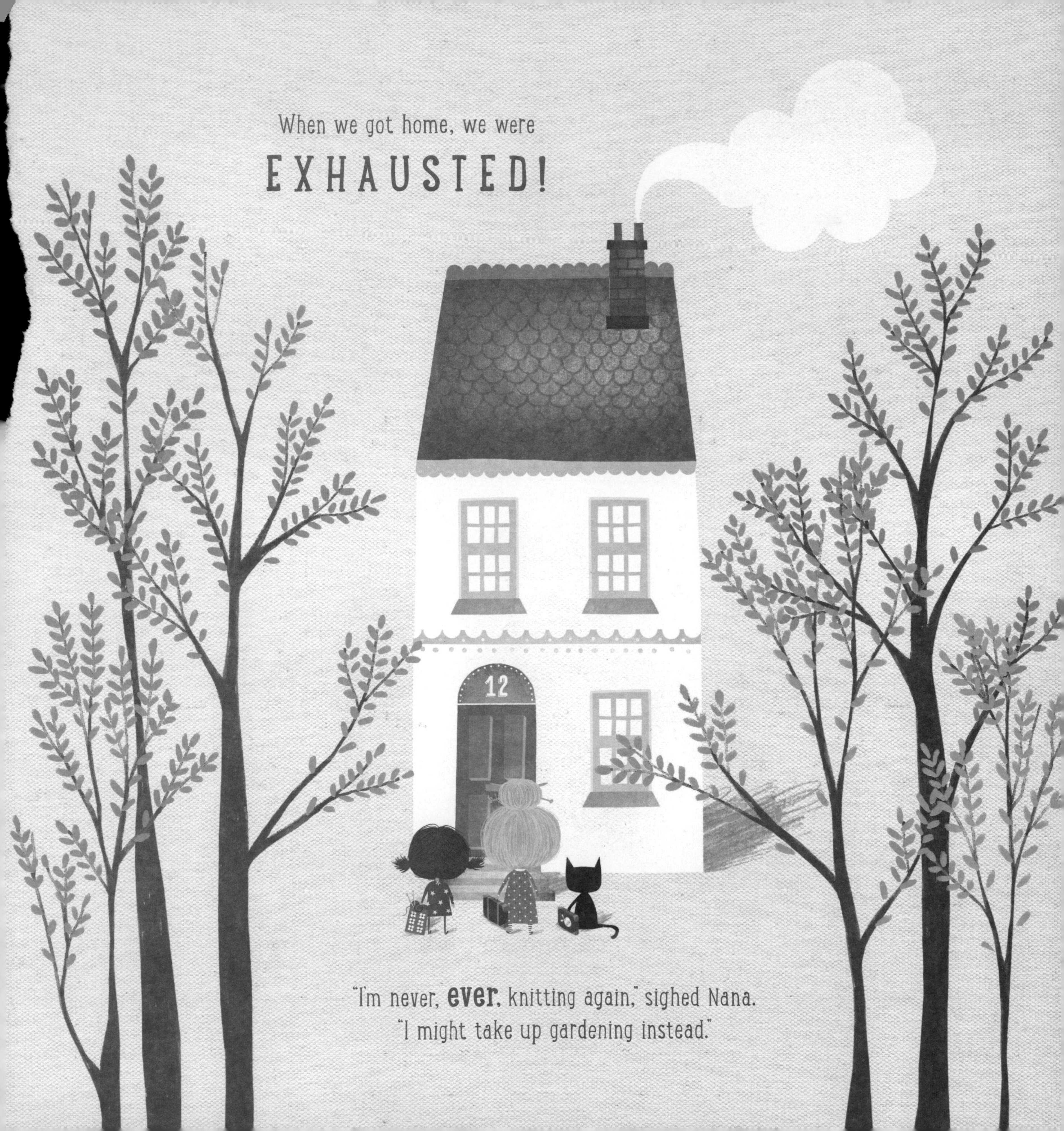

When we got home, we were

EXHAUSTED!

"I'm never, **ever**, knitting again," sighed Nana.
"I might take up gardening instead."

As we sat down for tea, I spluttered,
"**Urgh!** My drink's gone cold!"

"Don't worry," said Nana. "I know **just** what to do"...

...and she reached for her
needles and wool.